Must Be Christmas!

Text   Marlet Ashley
Illustrations   Kate Brown

Publisher - Ashley Brown Books

www.ashleybrownbooks.com

Must Be Christmas!

Revelry on the Estuary Series
Other books by Marlet Ashley and Kate Brown

  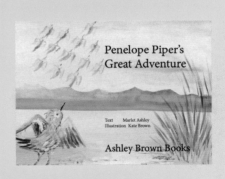

1. *The Interlopers*
ISBN 978-0-9879735-0-4

2. *Trumpeters' Tribulations*
ISBN 978-0-9879735-1-1

3. *Penelope Piper's Great Adventure*
ISBN 978-0-9879735-2-8

Publisher Ashley Brown Books
www.ashleybrownbooks.com

Marlet Ashley is a long-time educator with an M.A. in English Literature and Creative Writing from the
University of Windsor. She has taught creative writing at the University of Windsor and instructed literature and composition at Kwantlen Polytechnic University.

Her publications include a number of short stories and poetry in a variety of literary publications. In 2005, Marlet authored the Canadian edition of *Literature and the Writing Process* published by Pearson Prentice Hall, Toronto.

Born in Windsor, Ontario, she moved to Vancouver, BC in 1995. She presently lives with her husband Pieter Molenaar in Comox, British Columbia, close to the Comox Estuary.

Kate Brown developed a career as an interior designer, product designer and apparel designer.

In recent years Kate has been involved in story telling by designing museum exhibits.

Kate became aware of the wealth of stories of the everyday adventures of wild life on the Comox Estuary where she now lives. This motivated her to develop stories for *Revelry on the Estuary.*

Must Be Christmas!

"It must be Christmas," cried Taylor as she looked out the kitchen window.

"Almost," said her mother, who was busy doing the dinner dishes, but how can you tell?

"The swans are coming back," said Taylor, "Look!"

And sure enough, three wedges of trumpeter swans were flying low in the sky, getting ready to land in fields near the estuary.

"The swans always come back for Christmas."

With that, Taylor jumped from her chair, took down her coat, hat, and bright red scarf, put on her mitts, and ran out the door.

Outside, she heard the loud trumpeting of the swans as they drew closer and closer.

They were so beautiful that Taylor wanted to run up to them as they landed and welcome them back with a big hug.

The swans landed in the fields, hundreds of beautiful white trumpeters, and by tomorrow, Taylor knew, there would be hundreds more.

She watched the swans until she was called in for bed.

As her mother tucked her in, she told Taylor all about the trumpeter swans and how important it was to keep them safe so they would return again and again.

That night, Taylor dreamed of the beautiful birds and of Christmas.

Landing in the fields near the Comox Estuary were Sally and Samuel Swan and their young cygnet, Stella-Rose, a lovely and graceful little swan.

The small family was very tired after its long flight from the North, and to settle little Stella-Rose to sleep, her mother told her about the Comox Estuary, the place where they had landed. She told Stella-Rose the food was plentiful and the humans were kind.

"Before too long," her mother said, "the humanssss will light up their townssss with millionssss of light-ssss." She told Stella-Rose that soon the streets and trees would be twinkling brightly and that this time of year was called Christmas.

That night, Stella-Rose slept peacefully and dreamed of the beautiful lights, the kind humans, and of something called Christmas..

The same night, while Taylor and Stella-Rose were sleeping, snow began to fall. By the next morning, it was very hard to see the white swans in the deepening drifts.

Taylor thought how cold they must be. From her yard, she looked out onto the field and saw the little cygnet, Stella-Rose, tucked in close to her mother.

"She will freeze in the cold," Taylor said out loud, wondering what she might do to help.

Then, Taylor had an idea. She ran back into the house and gathered bits and boxes from the kitchen, attic and garage. She ran outside to the tall grasses and rushes that stood along a frozen stream close to her house. She worked very hard all day.

Later, just before supper when the day was becoming a little dark, a soft glow from the place where Taylor worked could be seen from the kitchen window.

"Whatever is she up to," Taylor's mother wondered, and she called for her husband to come outside with her.

The two of them walked out to the field to see what was keeping Taylor so very busy and what was creating such a lovely light.

And what they saw was a wonderful sight to behold!

Taylor had collected pine cones and tucked them in among the branches of the little evergreen. Draped across the tree were garlands of braided grasses and rushes. Little balls of suet and some dried apples hung here and there. And her own red scarf hung as a wreath in the centre of the pretty Christmas tree.

Flashlights, big and small, stood in the snow. They shone brighly as they circled the beautiful little tree and all of its decorations, especially Taylor's bright red wreath.

Two deer drew near, and a little rabbit hopped toward the lovely little tree, but the most amazing of all was the family of swans—a mother, father, and young one, Stella-Rose—who had come close, curious about the glow of lights and the little girl who was working so hard.

Taylor stood back to look at what she had made.

"How beautiful," said her mother.

"Good job," her father said.

Taylor stepped between them, and the little gathering of people, animals, and birds stood quietly admiring the beautiful tree.

Then, very slowly and quite nervously, the little swan, Stella-Rose, drew close to the tree. She pecked at a ball of suet just enough to cause the red-wreath scarf to gently fall from the branches and loosely tuck itself around Stella-Rose's graceful neck.

"She will be warm now," Taylor whispered to her mother, happy that she could give such a gift to the young swan.

Stella-Rose turned to her parents and whispered to her mother, "It musssst be Chrisssstmassss."

And it was.

Merry Christmas!

visit us again at

Ashley Brown Books

www.ashleybrownbooks.com

Made in the USA
Charleston, SC
12 November 2012